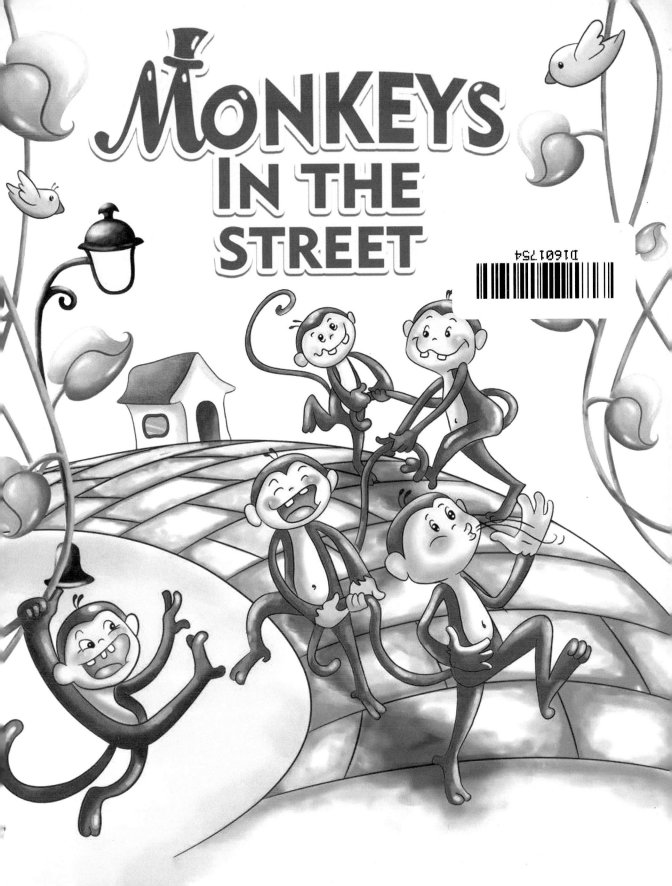

Monkeys in the Street

Stony Meadpow Publishing
Clearwater, Florida

This morning I rolled out of bed
And peeked out through the curtain.
I saw a monkey in the street
Of this I am quite certain.

My mouth dropped open (wouldn't yours?)
Imagine my surprise!
To see a monkey in the street
Right before my eyes.

I held my breath, I peeked again.
Did I live in a zoo?
I saw two monkeys in the street
That's right, not one, but two!

I blinked my eyes, I blinked them twice
I blinked them two times more.
There were monkeys in the street
Right outside my door!

Dad was snoring (what a noise!)
He woke from slumber deep.
He said "How grand, how very nice,
Now please just let me sleep."

I ran back to my window quick
(Afraid what I might see)
Yes, I saw more monkeys there
Not one, not two, but three!

I tried to wake my sister,
She mumbled as she woke.
She grumbled "It's too early!
It's too early for a joke!"

I raced into the living room
I peeked out of the door.
Yes, there were more monkeys there
Not two, not three -- but four!

Mom was in the kitchen,
Cooking eggs and bacon.
She said "That's just not possible,
I'm sure that you're mistaken."

I shook my head, I went outside,
I crept out to the drive.
And counted monkeys in the street.
One two, three, four, ... five!

I found Grampa in the backyard
I told him what was wrong.
He laughed and told me 'bout a fish
He'd caught that was t-h-i-s long!

I thought I'd take just one more look
(Perhaps they would be gone.)
And I would see no monkeys there
Not on the street or lawn.

I slowly peeked around the house
Were my eyes playing tricks?
There were monkeys, oh my gosh!
Two, three, four, five... six!

I knew I had to look once more
Would there be seven, eight or nine there?
Monkeys standing in the street
Standing in a line there?

There were monkeys everywhere
I tell you there were plenty!
Maybe ten, eleven, twelve,
Maybe even twenty!

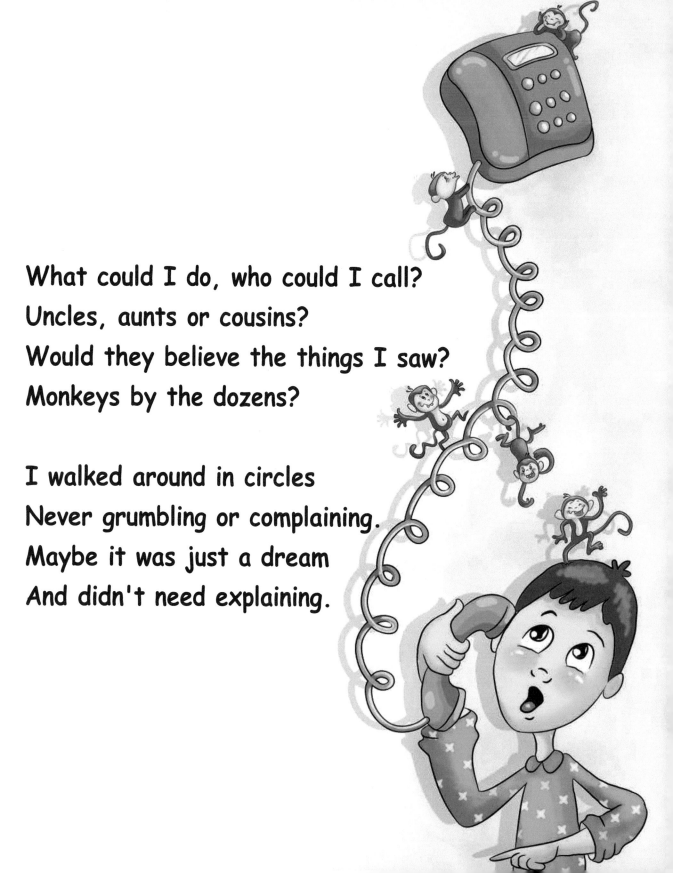

What could I do, who could I call?
Uncles, aunts or cousins?
Would they believe the things I saw?
Monkeys by the dozens?

I walked around in circles
Never grumbling or complaining.
Maybe it was just a dream
And didn't need explaining.

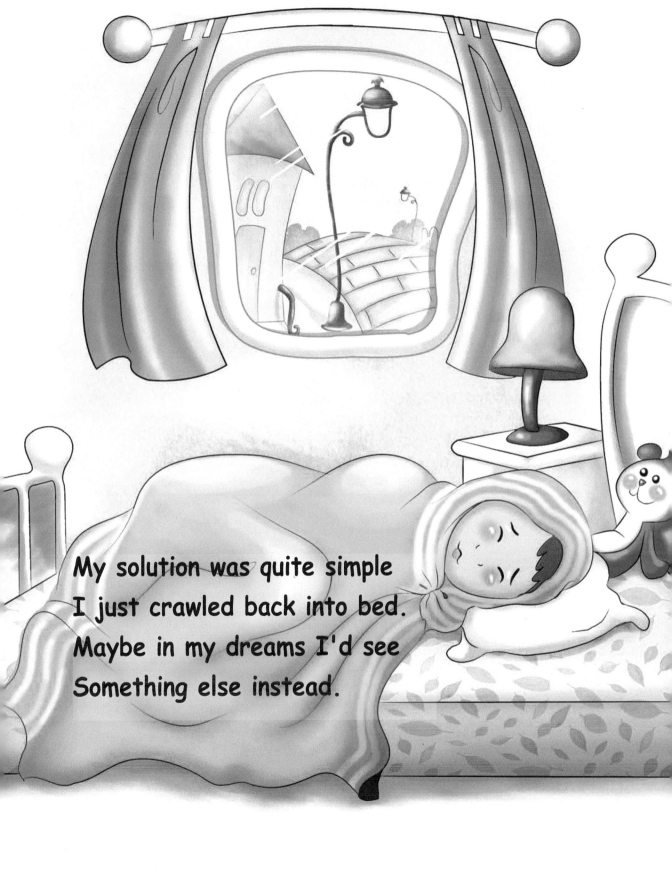

My solution was quite simple
I just crawled back into bed.
Maybe in my dreams I'd see
Something else instead.

I woke again much later
I looked into the yard.
There were no monkeys anywhere!
(And I looked very hard.)

There were not five, there were not four,
There were not two or three.
No, not a single monkey there
As far as I could see!

You can't imagine my relief
No monkeys anywhere!
I clapped my hands, I grinned, I laughed
I did a dance right there.

I played all day and half the night
And never saw a sign.
No monkeys in the street or yard
Not one, not ninety-nine!

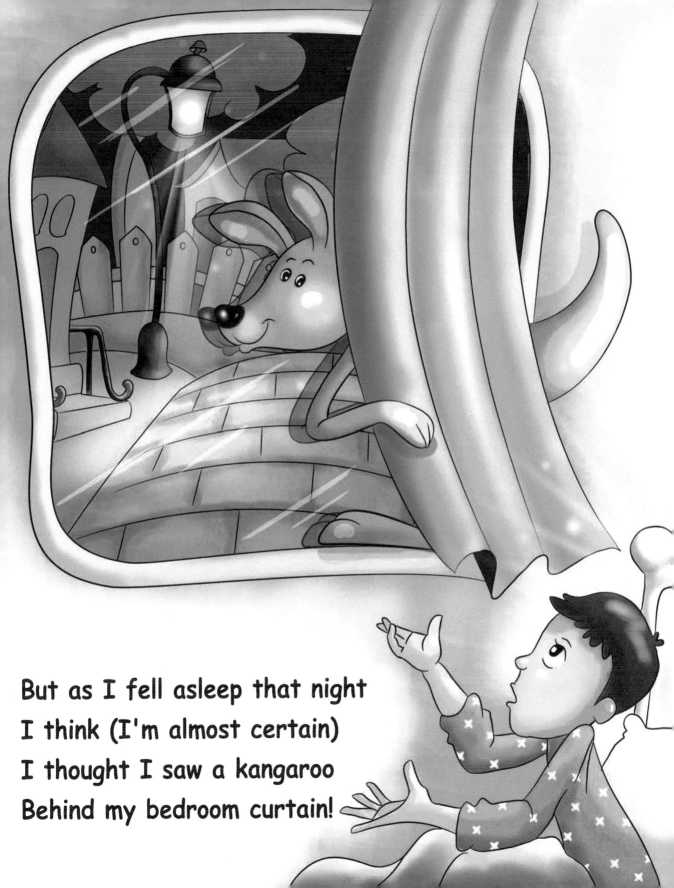

But as I fell asleep that night
I think (I'm almost certain)
I thought I saw a kangaroo
Behind my bedroom curtain!

Made in the USA
Columbia, SC
08 June 2024

36849488R00015